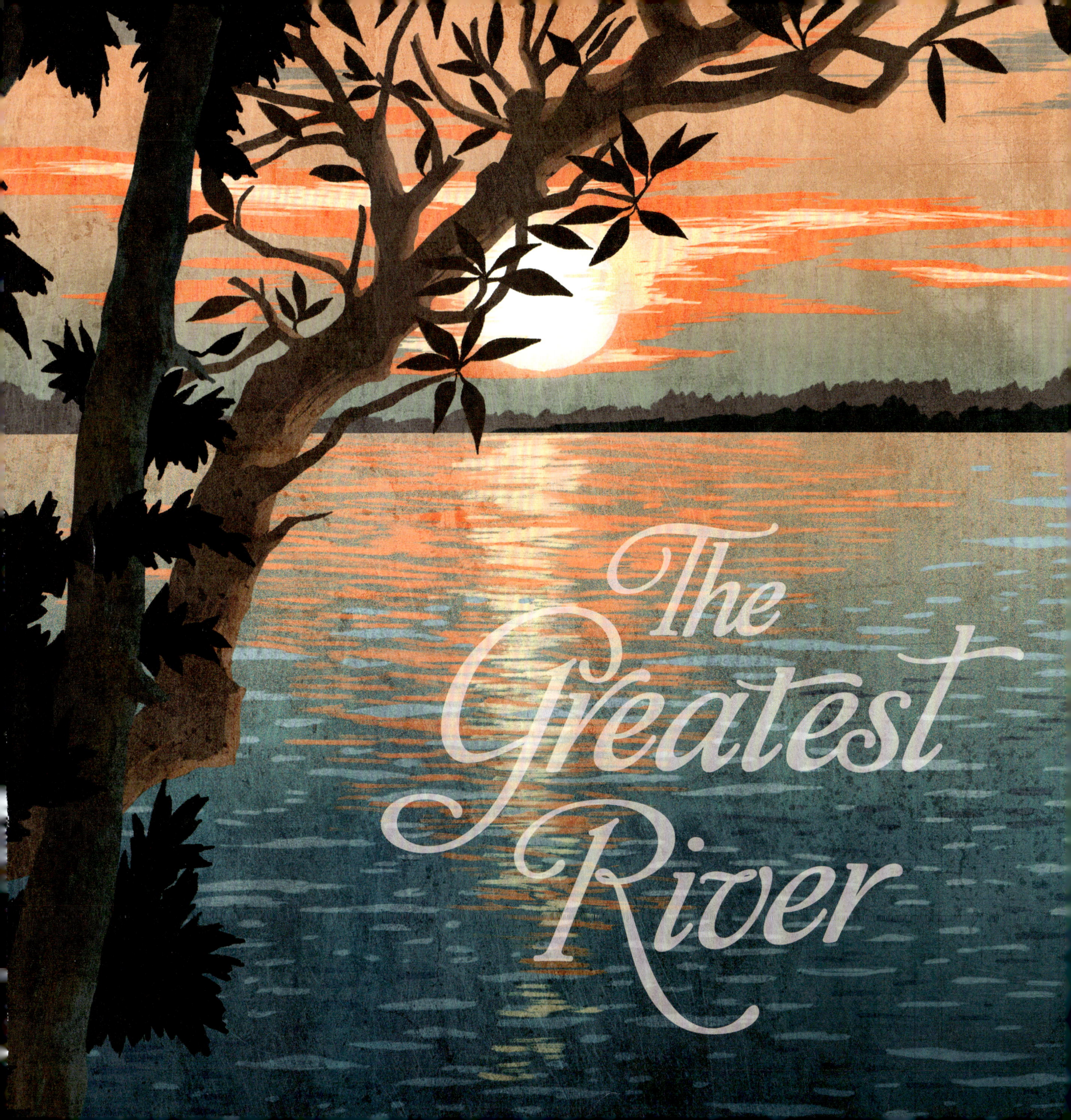

To Mamma and Sam Maasi. Thank you for being my greatest strength.—N.M.

For Shi. I hope we'll meet again in this great river.—K.L.

The Greatest River • Text copyright © 2025 by Namita Moolani Mehra • Illustrations copyright © 2025 by Khoa Le • All rights reserved. Manufactured in Capriate San Gervasio, Italy. • No part of this book may be used or reproduced in any manner whatsoever without written permission except in the case of brief quotations embodied in critical articles and reviews. For information address HarperCollins Children's Books, a division of HarperCollins Publishers, 195 Broadway, New York, NY 10007. • www.harpercollinschildrens.com • Library of Congress Control Number: 2022930786 • ISBN 978-0-06-320745-5 • Typography by Chelsea C. Donaldson • 24 25 26 27 28 RTLO 10 9 8 7 6 5 4 3 2 1 • First Edition

The Greatest River

by Namita Moolani Mehra

illustrated by Khoa Le

HARPER
An Imprint of HarperCollinsPublishers

Ever since Ananda was a baby,
her mamma had told her over and over again
about the magic of Ganga, the holy river.
Born in a glacier, high up in the Himalayas.
A river worshipped by millions.
A goddess.

"Ganga knows everything," Mamma always said. "She's the greatest mother of all."

Mamma talked endlessly about Ganga— more so after she got sick.

Ananda didn't understand how a river could be a great mother.
But now, standing at the banks of Ganga
with Mamma's sister, Maasi,
it was time to find out.

Time to experience the goddess's greatness,
bathe in her healing waters,
and pray for Mamma.

Maasi squeezed Ananda's hand

as they descended slippery, mossy stairs.

Freezing water numbed Ananda's feet,

yet all she felt was Ganga's warm embrace,

like the comfort of Mamma's arms.

A place where she could let go.

As Ganga gushed and swirled around her,
Ananda stood strong and still.
Breathe in. Breathe out.

Together they lit diyas that danced down the river, while chanting Mamma's favorite prayer.
Ganga listened.

Will Mamma be well again?
A glimmer of hope flickered inside Ananda.
Fears faded into the brilliant blue.
Sadness floated away.
Ganga understood.

The ride across the river was short,
but Ananda captured every moment:
Ganga shimmering in the late afternoon sun.
A million floating diamonds.
The misty air playing with Ananda's hair
and thanking her for coming.
Ananda hadn't smiled like that in a long time.

On the other side
stood ancient temples and ashrams.
Ananda heard familiar bhajans,
devotional songs Mamma often sang.

Heads swayed, voices connected, the earth hummed.
Ananda closed her eyes and felt the healing energy.
Maasi wept silently.

"It feels good to let it all out," she said.

Ananda hugged her tight.

After the evening aarti ceremony,
they walked to a small, hidden beach.

Sitting still with nature
offered a meditative moment
for Ananda to reflect.

Ananda wrote Mamma's name in the sand.
Ganga glistened.

Ananda admired the smooth and shiny river stones.

Each pebble more perfect than the next.

Each a solid thing to hold on to.

May I take one for Mamma?

Ganga gurgled.

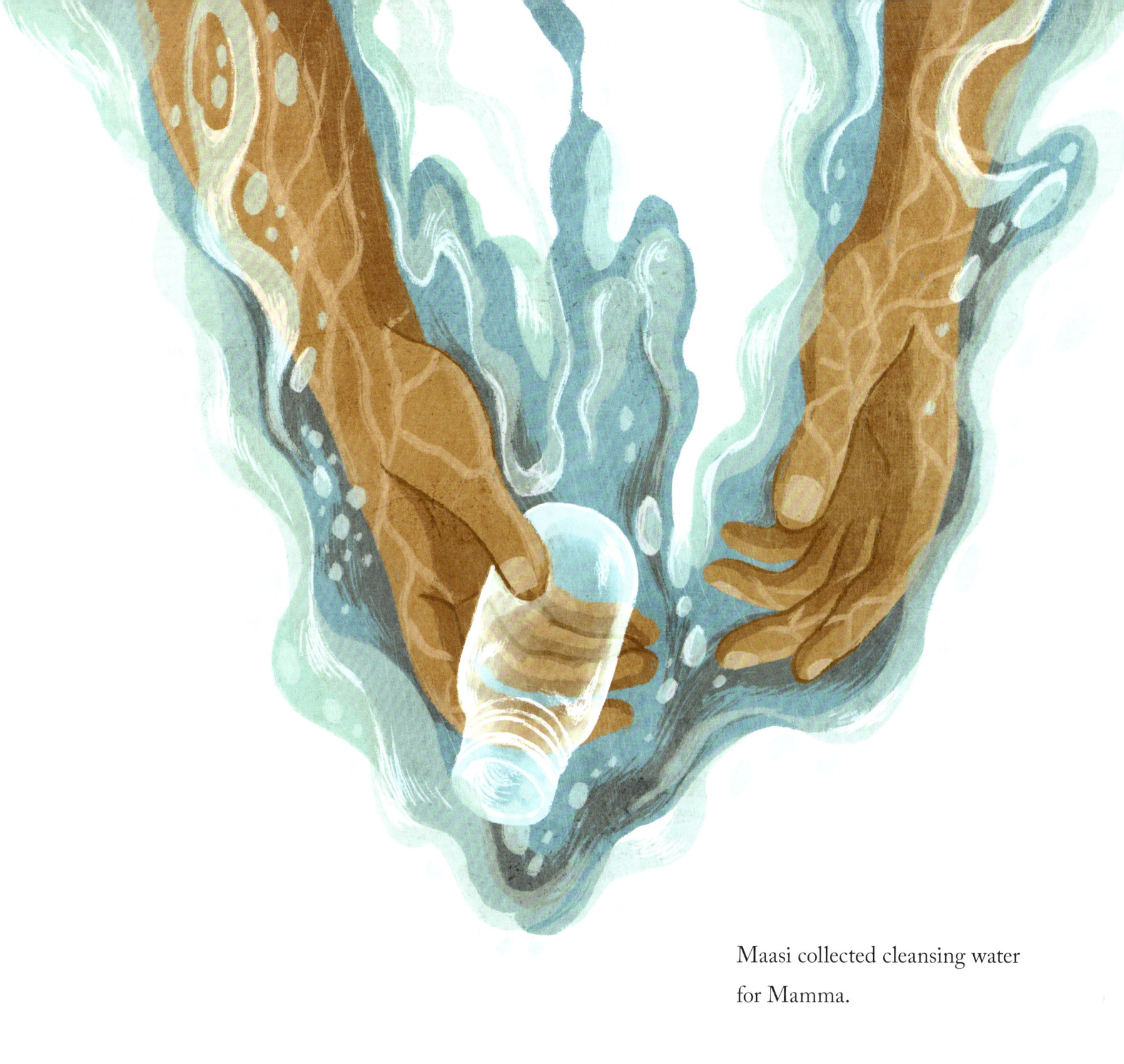

Maasi collected cleansing water for Mamma.

Ganga glowed.

They stayed until the sun sank low,
listening as temple bells rang,
white water rafters cheered,
rapids roared.

A river rhapsody—
sacred,
graceful,
powerful.

Ananda inhaled deeply.

She closed her eyes and took it all in.

The smells—incense, flowers, burning wood.

The sounds—chanting, singing, Ganga flowing.

The feeling—absolute peace.

Ananda memorized this magical scene and held it carefully in her mind's eye, where it would replay a thousand times.

The path ahead would be long and winding, like this great river.

But the might of Ganga was with her now.
Ananda exhaled slowly
as she walked away
from this great mother to her own.

Author's Note

Like many Indian children, I grew up listening to stories about Ganga. But it wasn't until my thirtieth birthday that I finally got to see the great river for myself. I flew from New York to India, where my mom and I journeyed into the mountains to spend a week at a yoga ashram. One evening, Mom took me to Haridwar, a holy town on the river, to watch the famous evening prayer ceremony. At first I was overwhelmed by the crowds, the chaos, and the commotion, but then I found myself in absolute awe of Ganga. The air was filled with temple bells ringing and devotional singing—all for Goddess Ganga. I felt an immediate and deep connection with this great river that everyone called Ma.

The next day, we found a quieter spot along the river, where I took my first dip in the glacial waters. It was freezing yet freeing. . . . I felt energized and alive!

Experiencing the force of Ma Ganga for the first time, with my mom, was special and meaningful.

In the years following this epic trip, Mom was diagnosed with a chronic illness, underwent multiple surgeries, and faced many health challenges.

More than a decade after my first visit to the holy river, my sister (whom my children call Maasi) and I had the opportunity to visit Ganga again.

On one particularly spectacular evening at the river, a radiant diya seller and her daughter helped us float lamps on the river. A stunning boat ride across Ganga led us to an emotional sunset prayer ceremony.

The next day, we visited a quiet, sandy beach by Ganga and collected pebbles as white-water rafters floated by.

Each moment at the holy river felt transformative, healing, and meditative.

The magical memories of Ganga fill my mind when I need them most, helping me focus, reset, and feel calmer. All I have to do is close my eyes, breathe deeply, and visualize the river.

I could never have imagined that a river would give me such strength and positivity during stressful times in my life. Nature has a wonderful power to heal.

Take a moment to sit in a quiet place and close your eyes. Think about something special and meaningful in nature that fills you with hope and joy. It could be a tree in your garden, an outdoor activity you enjoy doing, a place you once visited, or a special memory.

What image comes to mind that makes you feel calm and happy?

What is your Ganga?

Glossary

aarti—Hindu prayer ceremony

ashram—a place for spiritual and yoga practice

bhajans—songs with religious or spiritual words and meaning

diya—a clay or mud lamp with a cotton wick soaked in oil/ghee, lit to offer prayers

maasi—mother's sister; aunt

Cultural Note

Ganga (pronounced as GANG-AH), also known in the Western world as the Ganges, is the most important river in India. Ganga is considered to be sacred and is worshipped by many as the goddess of creation and abundance. She is often referred to as Ma or Mother.

Running nearly sixteen hundred miles long and winding through India and Bangladesh, Ganga originates from Gangotri, one of the largest glaciers in the Himalayas. Despite the freezing temperature of the water, millions of people take a dip in Ganga every single day as a holy ritual to spiritually cleanse themselves, seek blessings, and honor their faith. Ganga water is often used to purify, sprinkled by priests in prayer ceremonies and offered to the sick for healing.

Ganga is a symbol of faith, hope, and culture. At the same time, the great river of India is a source of income for hundreds of millions of people, putting a great deal of stress on the river, which is extremely littered and polluted in many parts. Hundreds of organizations, and even the Government of India, have invested time and money to clean up Ganga, but much work remains to be done to restore the holy river to literal purity.